Louise Leblanc

Leo and Julio

Illustrations by Philippe Brochard

Translation by Sarah Cummins

First Novels

Formac Publishing Company Limited
Halifax, Nova Scotia

Formac Publishing Company Limited acknowledges the support of the Nova Scotia Department of Tourism and Culture. We acknowledge the financial support of the Government of Canada through the Book Publishing Industry Development Program (BPIDP) Canadä for our publishing activities. We acknowledge the support of the Canada Council for the Arts for our publishing program.

Canadian Cataloguing in Publication Data

Leblanc, Louise, 1942-

    [Deux amis dans la nuit. English]

    Leo and Julio

    (First novel series)

    Translation of: Deux amis dans la nuit.

ISBN 0-88780-478-0 (pbk.)
ISBN 0-88780-479-9 (bound)

I. Cummins, Sarah. II. Brochard, Philippe, 1957-III. Title. IV. Series

PS8573.E25D4813   1999   jC843'.54   C99-950191-7 PZ7.
L4693Le 1999

Formac Publishing
Company Limited
5502 Atlantic Street
Halifax, NS B3H 1G4

Distributed in the U.S. by
Orca Book Publishers
P.O. Box 468 Custer, WA
U.S.A. 98240-0468

Printed and bound in Canada.

Table of Contents

The message

I have the coolest friend! He's a vampire. His name is Julio. He lives with his parents in an underground apartment in the cemetery. I met him by chance when I was visiting my grandfather's grave.

The only problem is we can't get together very often. Julio can't go outside in the daytime because the sunlight would kill him. And our friendship is a secret. If anyone else were to find out about Julio and his parents, their safety would be threatened.

Julio and I keep in touch with messages that we leave on my grandfather's grave. In his last note, Julio told me that his parents had gone out of town for a couple of days.

At last we'll get to see each other! I immediately fired off this message:

My parents are going out tomorrow evening. Please come

over to my house. Hide in the backyard at 7:15. I'm looking forward to a super fun evening with you!

Leo

1
Julio, where are you?

It's now 7:30! Great leaping french fries, was I ever worried! I thought my parents would never leave. My mother was in a state. This is the first time she's left me all alone at home.

"Now remember, don't let anyone in the house!"

"Who would come, Mom? Everyone in the village will be down at city hall with you and Dad."

"The neighbour is going to stop by in an hour," my dad informed me, "to make sure that nothing has happened to you."

Oh no! Now my evening with Julio will be ruined!

"I'm not going to get sick in the next hour! I don't want the neighbour to come by. He'll make me listen to his boring old stories."

"Did you invite someone over, by any chance?" My dad was suddenly suspicious. "One of your classmates?"

"A classmate? No! I invited over a VAMPIRE! And he'll eat the neighbour right up!"

Inside I was laughing at my clever deception. No way would my parents believe me. They just kept on telling me what not to do.

Don't cook anything! Not even hot chocolate. Don't light the stove. Don't play with matches. Don't make a fire in the fireplace. Blah blah blah.

I told them that I wasn't cold. I wasn't hungry, and I would drink nothing but water all evening long. Cross my heart and hope to die! Then I spat, to seal the deal.

They told me I had very bad manners. Finally they left.

As their car pulled out of the driveway and turned on to the street, I ran to my bedroom and opened the window.

"Julio! Where are you?"

No answer. Julio should be there! Maybe he didn't get my message. That would be so disappointing!

"Julio! Julio!"

"Shh! Here I am, Leo."

Julio stepped out from behind

the fir tree by the lake. He ran to the house and climbed over the windowsill. He was trembling.

"Don't be afraid. There's no one else at home."

"I was afraid when I was outside."

"Were you followed? Did anyone see you?"

"Lots of people saw me! Even though it was dark, I was terrified."

"I'll bet!"

"When you're different, you think that everyone is looking at you. I thought I would be found out. It was like I had the word VAMPIRE written on my forehead."

"Well, you're safe and sound now, that's the important thing. And we're together."

"Yeah, our first real evening together," said Julio, hugging me.

I could feel his heart racing. Not out of fear this time, but from excitement and happiness. My heart was beating fast too.

"I'll show you around the house. Then when you're at your house you can imagine being here."

DING DONG! DING DONG!

Great leaping french fries! Not the neighbour already!

2
Hop to it, twerp!

Julio was so frightened he wanted to leave right away. But I reassured him. I told him old Mr. Applebaum would not come into my room.

"I'll get rid of him and then I'll be right back. Wait for me, promise?"

"Cross my heart and hope to die," he promised, with a little smile.

Poor Julio. It's no picnic being a vampire. It's hard when you're different.

I looked at my watch. It was 8:05. The neighbour was early.

I hoped he wasn't planning on hanging around.

DING DONG! DING DONG!

What a pain! Hold your horses, neighbour.

"Listen, Mr. Appleb—"

"Hi there, pinhead!"

"B...B...Butch!"

Butch is a big kid from school. He's a bully. He loves to bug little kids and hurt them. Lately he's been picking on me.

Before I could get over my stupefaction, Butch had stepped into the house. He shut the door behind him.

"See, I've been thinking of you, twerp. You know what I thought? I thought you'd be lonely, all alone in this great big house."

"I'm not alone! I have a babysitter!"

"Ha ha ha! Don't kid me. I know there's no babysitter."

"How do you know? I do so have a babysitter!"

"Don't get smart with me, kiddo. Your mom phoned my mom, that's how I know. It was her last hope of finding someone. So get this straight, twerp, I know everything about you!"

Great leaping french fries! Butch has discovered my secret. He must have followed Julio. He knows Julio is here. No, he doesn't! He thinks I'm alone. Stay cool, Leo.

Butch started toward the living room.

"This is a pretty nice place, twerp. I bet your bedroom is really nice too. You must have a lot of really nice things that I might be interested in!"

My bedroom! He must not go into my bedroom! Suppose I told him there was a vampire in there? No good. He would just laugh. Anyway, the vampire would be afraid of Butch, not the other way around. I have to keep him away from the bedroom!

"But first, I want you to show me the kitchen!"

I was so surprised that I couldn't move. Butch must have thought I was refusing to show him the kitchen.

"Hop to it, twerp!" he growled, "or I'll pulverize you!"

Acting as if I was terrified of him, I led Butch to the kitchen. He had no idea how pleased I really was. I can tell you, I was really frightened for a moment there.

"I want something to warm me up," announced Butch.

"Warm you up? Sorry, I promised my mom I wouldn't light anything."

"Ha ha! You always make me laugh, little Leo. That's what I like about you. Ha ha!"

"What did I say that's so funny?"

"Maybe I can get lit without lighting anything! Ha ha ha!"

I still couldn't understand why the big bully was laughing so hard. While he was chuckling, I checked the time. 8:20. The neighbour would be by in ten minutes. I would have to keep Butch in the kitchen until then.

"I don't want anything to eat. I want something to drink."

"Okay. Well, there's milk, and—"

"Ha ha! Milk! Ha ha ha!"

Why was he laughing like that? Well, go ahead, you big turkey, laugh all you want. While you're laughing, time is passing.

"Milk? Are you out of your tiny mind, pinhead? Milk won't warm me up. Now get out of the way!"

Butch pushed past me and opened the fridge. It was 8:26.

"Now here's what I want!"

Then he took a beer out of the fridge! He sat down and put his feet up on the table. He opened the bottle. I was flabbergasted.

"You're impressed, eh, twerp? Well, when you're my age..."

Butch is 14. He thinks he's a man. But he's just an idiot who's wrecking his health. I could tell him he's heading for an early grave, but he would only laugh.

Anyway, I hope he does die young. Very young, like now, at 8:29.

"Hey, Leo, you've been going to the cemetery a lot these days. I've seen you."

"I...I'm visiting my grandfather."

"Visiting a dead guy? Every day? Do you think I'm crazy? You'll have to think of something better than that!"

Butch got up. Wow, he's tall! I took a step back, glancing at my watch. It was 8:30.

Please, please be on time, Mr. Applebaum, I beg you! I'll never again say that you're a boring old windbag. I'll listen to all your stories for hours on end. Just come! Ring the bell!

DING DONG!

"What? Who's that?" said Butch nervously, putting down his beer.

"It's my babysitter, Butch. Mr. Applebaum. You remember him. He used to be a cop."

"Applebaum? That old guy?"

"Yeah, but a big old guy."

"Okay, okay, I don't want any problems with the police."

Butch opened the door to the backyard. Hopefully, Julio had not decided to hide out there!

"I'm not finished with you, Leo," sneered Butch. "Remember, not a word about my little visit."

Once he was outside, I gathered the courage to answer back.

"You make me laugh, Butch. Now hop to it!"

I watched him as he walked away along the shore. When I closed the door I began to shake. Only then did I fully realize the danger I had been in.

DING DONG! DING DONG!

3
They're so blue, Leo!

I should have greeted Mr. Applebaum with open arms. But I was thinking of Julio. Every minute that went by made our time together shorter. One down, one to go!

"Listen, Mr. Applebaum..."

"You took your time answering the door!"

"I... I fell asleep in my bedroom."

"So did I," he answered, stepping inside.

He was shivering. He had on his dressing gown. Great leaping french fries, was he going to spend the night here?

"I promised your parents I would stop by, but I can't stay. I'm not feeling well."

"You're sick? That's great... uh, greatly disappointing."

"Everything's all right here? You seem kind of nervous."

"Nervous? Oh yes! I'm always nervous. It's just my temperament, as my mother says."

"Well, all right then. I'll just be getting back to bed."

"That would be the best thing... for you, Mr. Applebaum."

Hooray, he was gone! I rushed to my bedroom. But Julio wasn't there!

Then I heard a creak. The closet door opened, slowly, and Julio

appeared. Like a ghost he glided to my bed and sat down.

"What an evening. It'll be a miracle if I don't die of fright!" he whispered.

"The next-door neighbour has gone home to bed but Butch thinks he's still here. Nobody else will come."

"Are you sure? Because if I hear ding-dong one more time, I'll go ding-dong!"

We both burst out laughing. How you can laugh so much at such a stupid joke, I don't know. But sometimes it's fun to be stupid.

Suddenly I stopped laughing. It was 8:45. Julio had to leave in forty-five minutes!

"I had a present for you, but it's too late. No! I can still give you a little bit."

"Give me a little bit of present?"

I led Julio out into the hall and to the living room.

"There sure are a lot of doors in your place," Julio remarked. "It's huge. And that window there is gigantic. You can see—"

He stopped. I immediately panicked. Was Butch back?

"What? What can you see?"

"Everything! The trees and the lake. It's as if nature comes right into the house. It must be even more beautiful in the day-time."

I breathed a little easier.

"I envy you," said Julio sadly.

"I know, Julio. Ever since I've known you I've realized how lucky I am to live in freedom and to enjoy even the simplest things. That's what I wanted to give you for a present."

I showed him a video of beautiful landscapes.

"I wanted to give you colour, so you would see something different from the grey shades of night. I wanted to show you the real colour of things, like you've never seen before. Daylight colours."

"I mustn't." Julio was worried. "My parents don't want me to see that. They want to protect me, to make sure I won't be tempted to go out during the daytime."

"You can still dream! Your parents can't stop you from dreaming. You know yourself better than they do. Would you go outside in the daytime and put your life at risk?"

Julio wasn't sure what to say.

"Sometimes I wish Butch would die," I told him. "I would gladly strangle him. But I don't want to ruin the rest of my life."

"All right," said Julio.

I slipped the cassette into the

VCR. Time had passed so quickly. It was already 9:10. I advanced the film to show Julio the best parts. First he blinked, but then his eyes stayed wide open.

On the screen we saw the sea and then a mountain rising in the gloom. A fireball slowly climbed up the side of the

mountain. Then it broke free and floated into the sky like a golden balloon.

"The sun," murmured Julio. "Is that what a sunrise is like, Leo?"

"Yes, Julio."

Suddenly Julio put up his arms and shielded his face. He quickly lowered them again, realizing he didn't need to protect himself.

He watched as the rising sun awakened the blue of the sky and the sea, shedding its radiant light over everything.

"The sea and the sky are so blue, Leo. You could never imagine anything as beautiful as that."

"Wait! I want to show you something else!"

"No, I just want to see the sun again, and the day breaking."

Julio stared at the screen, fascinated. His eyes filled with tears. Then they began to change colour, turning bluer and bluer, as if they were drinking up the sea.

A drop of salt water slid down Julio's cheek, carrying in it the shining sun.

4
Leo, I want the truth!

I showed many other beautiful places to Leo. Every burst of colour sent him into raptures.

"Shh! I think I heard a noise. Great leaping french fries! My parents are back!"

Julio's terror paralyzed him. I shook him.

"Quick, go to my room."

He was off like a shot. I turned off the television and went to meet my parents. I was so nervous I started to hiccup.

"Hi, Mom... *hic*!"

"Is everything all right?" asked my dad. "Did Mr. Applebaum stop by?"

"Yep! Right on time! Boy, was I glad to see him!"

"I thought you didn't want him to come by."

"Um, anyway, he didn't stay long. He wasn't feeling well. Hic!"

"You don't look well yourself. You've got the hiccups. I bet you stuffed yourself with cookies."

"No! I didn't have any cookies! You always think the worst of me!"

"Okay, okay, we believe you! Why are you getting so upset?"

"I'll go make you some hot water with lemon," said my

mother. "Go get your pyjamas on."

I went out into the hall, turning back to see if my parents were following me.

BANG! I bumped into the basement door, which had been left open. My head throbbing, I

made my way to my room. There was no one there. Julio must have gone to hide in the garden.

I tried to open the window, but the safety catch was on. Julio couldn't have gone out that way! I looked under the bed, in the closet, in my toy chest. No Julio.

My thoughts were all mixed up. The only thing my head could come up with was a big lump where I had bumped it... on the basement door! Which was left open! Great leaping french fries! Julio had opened the wrong door!

I went down to the basement.

"I know you're down here, Julio. I'm going to lock the door. I'll come down again and let you out after my parents are asleep."

A muffled voice answered me.

"Don't abandon me, Leo."

"I won't. Cross my heart and hope to die."

It broke my heart to lock Julio up. I slipped the key into my pocket and went up to the kitchen. I felt much calmer. My parents didn't suspect a thing.

"LEO! I WANT THE TRUTH!"

My blood ran cold and started throbbing in my veins.

"What truth, Dad?"

"*The* truth! There's only one!"

I clutched the key hidden in my pocket, reminding myself that my parents suspected nothing. They couldn't have seen

Julio. They were thinking about something else. Cookies!

"I swear that I didn't eat any—"

"Forget the cookies!" my father exploded.

"You're not yourself," said my mother. "And now we know why."

So *I* exploded. It was the only way to hide how nervous I was.

"You don't know anything at all! I banged my head on the—"

Whoops! I didn't want to mention the basement!

"On a door. And that's why I'm not acting normal!"

"Are you sure? Or is it because of THIS?" asked my dad, in a furious voice.

The beer bottle! I didn't know what to say. I couldn't tell my

parents that Butch had been by. They would phone his parents and Butch would pulverize me.

"LEO! I asked you a question."

I was more frightened of Butch than of my parents. It was better to tell a lie.

"Okay, yes! It was me. I just wanted to taste it."

"Taste it! That was quite a big taste!" said my dad sarcastically. "The bottle is half empty. You're drunk!"

"Leo," said my mother, her voice trembling, "our little boy..."

My eyes filled with tears. This was too much!

"I'm not drunk!" I yelled. I jumped up, tripped over a chair, and sprawled on the floor.

"Go to bed, Leo," my dad said. "Your mother and I need to think about all this."

Painfully I got to my feet and went to my room thinking I had never had so many problems in my entire life.

5
Murderers!

I don't know what my parents decided, but they sure spent a long time talking about it. My eyelids grew heavy and I drifted off for a bit, I think. Then I woke up again.

I was totally alert. I couldn't hear a sound. It was safe to go and set Julio free. I got out of bed and tiptoed to the door. A few rays of light fell across the floor. That was weird!

Light was streaming through the blind. It couldn't be! I looked at the clock. 7:05.

I had slept through the night.

Julio! There was a window in the basement. He must be... dead! Killed by the light of day. And by me. It was my fault. My friend, my friend Julio...

Overcome with despair, I got back into bed. I was too afraid to go down to the basement. I could still hear Julio's muffled plea: "Don't abandon me, Leo."

My heart was heavy with grief. I burst into tears. I hid under the covers to muffle my...Wait!

Julio's voice had been muffled too! That meant he had hidden somewhere. In the cedar cupboard! Where there was no light. He was still alive!

Silently I got out of bed. I opened the bedroom door. Great leaping french fries! My parents

were in the hall. My mother was carrying a basket of dirty laundry and she was not in a good mood.

"I do *not* understand why the basement door is locked. And where is the key?"

"We can look for it after breakfast," said my father. "The laundry is not that urgent."

"Yes, it is," my mother replied impatiently. "I have several loads to do. And I want to take some winter clothes out of the cedar cupboard. The weather's getting colder now."

"All right," said my father. "There's an extra key in the kitchen. I'll go fetch it."

I felt every muscle in my body tighten in response to the possible danger. I could not escape. It was the moment of truth. The alternative was Julio's death. I had to save him.

I grabbed the key to the basement door and ran out of my room. I said good morning to my mother and opened the basement door. She dropped her laundry basket in astonishment.

Before she could get over her surprise, I ran down the stairs.

I could hear her hurried footsteps, then my dad's. They were coming downstairs. There they were, out of breath. They found me with my arms stretched out in front of the cedar cupboard.

"Will you please tell us what is going on?" my mother said in an exasperated tone.

"Y-y-you must not open this cupboard!"

"Why ever not?" she asked, astonished.

"It's simple," said my father. "There's someone in the cupboard."

My dad looked me straight in the eye.

"You invited someone over last night. The two of you opened a bottle of beer, and then we came home earlier than expected. You shut your friend up in the cupboard so we wouldn't find him. You thought you could let him out later, but..."

"This is very serious," exclaimed my mother. "This boy's

parents must be worried to death. Open the door, Leo."

"NO! I BEG YOU!" yelled Julio from inside the cupboard.

I yelled too. I cried out the truth like a desperate man.

"YES! YES! I invited a friend over. YES! I locked him in the cupboard. Because he's a vampire! If you open the door, he will die. The light will kill him. You will be *murderers!*"

My father held his head in his hands.

"Leo, do you think we'll believe such a story? Really, Leo, this is going too far. Step away from the door."

I raised my fists. My mother held my father back, murmuring, "I've never seen Leo in such a state. He is definitely very worried about something."

Then she spoke to me, in a gentle voice.

"Leo, you know you can always talk to us. You can trust us. Tell us what you think we should do."

I put my fists down and tried to think. My parents didn't believe me. The only one who could convince them was Julio.

"If you cover up the window," I said, "I'll open the cupboard door."

Grumpily, my father complied. He cut open a large cardboard box and taped it to the window. Then he turned on the light.

"Now," he said sharply, "you open that door!"

"Julio!" I said. "It's Leo. You can come out now. It's safe. Cross my heart and hope to die!"

Watching my parents' reaction, I opened the door a crack. I had the feeling they were beginning to believe me. They took a step backwards, as if they expected a monster to appear.

6
So it was all true!

"Thank you, Leo," said Julio as he stepped out of the cupboard. "You were great!"

Julio is really great! He walked over to my parents, holding out his hand.

"I'm very pleased to meet you both."

"See, you can tell he's a vampire! No kid from school would ever say that!"

"We can talk about it over breakfast," suggested my father, with a smile.

Great leaping french fries! He still didn't get it.

"I'm sorry," said Julio. "I can't leave this basement."

My mother got up and took my father by the arm, dragging him to the stairs.

"We'll bring breakfast down here," she said.

Julio was worried.

"Your parents don't believe us. What if they call the police?"

By the time I had managed to reassure him, my parents were back, carrying two trays of food. They were acting very strange.

"Eat up, kids! You must be hungry after all that excitement!"

Julio seemed to relax a bit.

"Tell us about yourself, Julio. What's it like to be a vampire?"

Julio explained that he lived with his parents in the cemetery, underneath the tomb of Orasul.

"I see," said my dad. "And are your parents at home right now?"

"They've gone to help out some other vampires who live in the next village. There are vampires in practically every cemetery, you know."

"Other vampires, of course," repeated my father. He didn't seem very surprised.

"You have a good appetite, Julio," remarked my mother. "I thought vampires only—"

"Drank blood." Julio laughingly finished her sentence. "Those are just tall tales, you know."

"Do you drink beer?" asked my father suddenly.

"I might be a vampire," exclaimed Julio, shocked, "but I'm not like that Butch!"

I practically choked on my bite of toast. Then I had to admit everything: Butch's visit, his threats, and my lie about the beer.

My parents are really weird. They didn't seem happy that I

hadn't drunk any beer. They didn't say a word about Butch. I guess nothing could surprise them now.

"If you could go home now," they asked Julio, "would you?"

"Of course!" he exclaimed. "My parents are supposed to phone me at noon. They'll be very worried if there's no answer."

"I can promise you," declared my mother. "You will be at the tomb of Orasul before noon. We've got it all figured out."

My parents smiled at one another. They looked like two kids planning something naughty. Julio and I looked like two worried parents. Everything was all mixed up!

* * *

Julio was covered up from head to toe. He was wearing gloves, dark glasses, and my ski mask which hid every square inch of his face. A blanket was draped over his shoulders.

Julio thought that the blanket was unnecessary, but my mother insisted.

"We mustn't take even the slightest risk, you know!" she said in a strange voice.

Then we got in the car and went to buy some flowers to put on my grandfather's grave.

Julio was very nervous when we got to the cemetery. He looked all around him.

My parents still didn't realize the gravity of the situation. They seemed to think it was amusing. They stopped at my grandfather's grave, but I pushed them on.

"We'll lay the flowers on the grave later."

Fortunately, there were no other people around.

When we got to Orasul's tomb, Julio thanked my parents and walked up the steps leading to the door. He took a kind of electronic remote control out of his pocket and opened the door.

I ran up after him. When he hugged me, I could feel his heart beating.

"My friend." That was all he said.

He handed the blanket to me and disappeared inside the tomb. As I went back down the steps I saw that my mother had dropped the bouquet of flowers for grand-dad. My father had turned as white as... as a vampire.

"So it really was true," he murmured. "He really is a—"

"V-v-vampire," stammered my mother. "Was it all true?

Butch, his threats, and the rest? Was that true too?"

Now I understand why my parents were acting that way! They didn't believe a word of my story!

They played along so they could prove that I had made it all up. But they got caught in their own trap! Now they were both petrified!

It really was a terrible shock for them. That night, they didn't sleep a wink.

And neither did I, because my mother called up Butch's mother. Just thinking of it makes my head pound! Great leaping french fries!

Three more new novels in the First Novels Series!

Maddie Tries to Be Good
b y Louise LeBlanc/ Illustrated by Marie-Louise Gay
When Maddie sets her heart on playing the role of the elephant in the school play, she decides the only way she's going to win the role is to behave very, very well. At first her brothers and her friends can hardly believe the change that's come over her, but eventually they come to accept the new Maddie. And Maddie learns that being thoughtful and considerate isn't quite as hard as she expected.

Marilou on Stage
by Raymond Plante/ Illustrated by Marie-Claude Favreau
Marilou's class is putting on a play, based on an old fable. Everyone has a role, and Marilou is the star. But no one likes the way the story turns out, until the class decides they can give the fable whatever ending they want. In their new version, everyone gets treated fairly.

Missing Mooch
by Gilles Gauthier/ Illustrated by Pierre-Andre Derome
Carl is on his way to his summer holidays on the Magdalen Islands. He remembers the islands as the place where he and his old dog Mooch had so much fun. This time Carl is going with his friend Gary and Gary's dog Dumpling. Terrified of everything, Dumpling clings tightly to Gary. Carl can't help remembering his noble and magnificent mooch, and how she protected the beach from seagulls and swam out fearlessly to fetch sticks. The more ridiculous Dumpling becomes, the more Carl is convinced that he has to do something to honour Mooch's life.

Meet all the great kids in the First Novels Series!

Arthur
Arthur Throws a Tantrum
Arthur's Dad
Arthur's Problem Puppy

Fred
Fred and the Food
Fred and the Stinky Cheese
Fred's Dream Cat

Leo
Leo and Julio
The Loonies

Loonie Summer
The Loonies Arrive

Maddie
Maddie in Trouble
Maddie Goes to Paris
Maddie in Danger
Maddie in Goal
Maddie wants Music
That's Enough Maddie!

Meet all the great kids in the First Novels Series!

Mikey
Mikey Mite's Best Present
Good For You, Mikey Mite!
Mikey Mite Goes to School
Mikey Mite's Big Problem

Mooch
Missing Mooch
Mooch Forever
Hang On, Mooch!
Mooch Gets Jealous
Mooch and Me

The Swank Twins
The Swank Prank
Swank Talk

Max
Max the Superhero

Will
Will and His World